Here's a story to share!

Sharing a story with your child is great fun and it's an ideal way to start your child reading.

The left-hand pages are 'your' story pages. The right-hand pages are specially written for your child with simple vocabulary and helpful repetition.

• Cuddle up close and look through the book together. What's happening in the pictures?

• Read the whole story to your child, both your story pages and your child's. Tell your child what it says on his* story pages and point to the words as you say them.

• Now it's time to read the story again and see if your child would like to join in and read his story pages along with you. Don't worry about perfect reading – what matters at this stage is having fun.

• It's best to stop when your child wants to. You can pick up the book at any time and enjoy sharing the story all over again.

Here the child is referred to as 'he'. All Ladybird books are equally suitable for both boys and girls.

Edited by Lorraine Horsley and Caroline Rashleigh
Designed by Alison Guthrie, Lara Stapleton and Graeme Hole

A catalogue record for this book is available from the British Library

Published by Ladybird Books Ltd
27 Wrights Lane London W8 5TZ
A Penguin Company

2 4 6 8 10 9 7 5 3 1

TEXT © JUDITH NICHOLLS MMI
ILLUSTRATIONS © LADYBIRD BOOKS LTD MMI

LADYBIRD and the device of a Ladybird are trademarks of Ladybird Books Ltd

Caterpillars can't fly!

by Judith Nicholls
illustrated by Cecilia Johansson

"Who is that?" asked the honeybee,
swooping from the summer sky.

"It can't be just a petal,
it's underneath that nettle,
and I really can't imagine why."

"It's a lump,
it's a clump.
I'm sure it couldn't jump,"
croaked the cricket as he flitted by.

"But, wait a minute,
I think there's something in it!
Wasn't that a wriggle?
I'm sure I saw it wiggle
from the corner of my eye!"

6

"It's a cluster in a fluster,"
laughed the lacewing,
hovering by the garden wall.

"It's a fluster of a cluster,"
laughed the ladybird,
"and it looks as if it wants to crawl!"

Soon the first drab grub
had struggled from her egg
and staggered over nettle,
till she caught a glimpse of sky.

And from that moment on,
though she nibbled and she spun,
she dreamt a silent dream
that she would take off to the sun;
she dreamt a secret dream
that she would fly.

"Can she dance?"
asked the dragonfly,
darting from her stream to the sky.

"She can wriggle, she can jiggle,"
giggled Lacewing. "She can nibble, she can
dribble – but I'm sure she'll never fly!"

11

"You can spin, you can run,"
huffed the honeybee,
buzzing as she passed close by.

"You can spin, you can run,
you can reach up for the sun,
but you're never going to fly.
You'd better settle on your nettle –
however hard you try
you are never going to fly!"

But the drab grub grew;
she grew and grew.
She no longer spun,
but her gaze stayed on the sun,
and she hung on to her dream
that she would fly.

She grew...

and she grew...

till she burst from her skin.

Then she grew even more
and did it all again –
and with each new skin
she dreamt that she would fly.

Then, one day she tired.
She crept away to hide,
to sleep beneath her nettle.
She crept beneath her nettle
and she slept.

"I see no wing," the dragonfly sang
and she raised her own to the sky.

"I see no wing," sang the cranefly.
"It's clear to me that thing
is never going to fly."

The sharp-eyed bee
buzzed a gentle lullaby;
the poppy-scarlet ladybird
proudly waved goodbye.

"Just settle on that nettle –
you are never going to fly."

But in the darkness
still she dreamed
a dream that would not die.

In the long dark night
of the chrysalis
she dreamt of sun and sky.

And then,

one day…

A split, a crack,
brought the dragonfly back
to see her struggle to a twig.

"Who are you?" puzzled Bee.
"You're a mystery to me!"

"A magician," murmured Lacewing,
"to be born again from that
strange egg!"

Then all of them saw the silent dream
that had gleamed before in her eye.

They watched her struggle on to
her twig…

They watched her spread herself
to dry.

They watched her raise
two rainbow wings
and reach for the sun
and the sky.

Turn off the TV, close the door, too.
Here's a story to share for just me and you...

Inky-pinky blot

Who is the inky-pinky blot in the dark, dark pond? He asks everyone who goes by, but no one ever seems to know...

Caterpillars can't fly!

A baby caterpillar dreams of flying high in the sky but all her friends just laugh. What is she to do?

By the light of the Moon

Charlie the zoo keeper has gone home and the zoo is quiet. Now it's time for the animals to dance by the light of the moon...

Molly Maran and the Fox

It's cold outside and Molly the kind-hearted hen says all the animals can stay in her warm barn. But how will she keep out the wily fox?